The Family Minus's
Summer House

Parents Magazine Press ❧ New York

The Family Minus's Summer House

FERNANDO KRAHN

Library of Congress Cataloging in Publication Data
Krahn, Fernando.   The family Minus's summer house.
SUMMARY: Harry Minus and his "numerous" family spend an
enjoyable day in the country, picnicking, admiring the scenery,
and putting up a portable tree house.
[1. Humorous stories]   I. Title. PZ7.K8585Fap [E]   78-23717
ISBN 0-8193-0991-5   ISBN 0-8193-0992-3 lib. bdg.

The Family Minus's
Summer House

The Family Minus went out for a drive in the country.
As they were riding up a bumpy road,
Harry Minus turned to his family and said,
"I have a big surprise for all of you."

Suddenly he stopped the car, climbed to the
top of a rock, and made his announcement.

"That tree you see down there
and all the hills around it belong to us.
I've bought them," he said.

The family rolled happily down the slope,

landing at the trunk of the tree.

"Oh, Harry, I like this place so much,"
said his wife, Mary.

"Yes," he answered, "it makes me very hungry.
Let's eat now!"

So together they carried the picnic basket
joyfully down the hill.

Harry spread the tablecloth while Mary
smiled proudly at the egg-peeler she recently invented.

Then the Minuses, in their age-old picnic tradition, made grilled sausages and onion salad.

Also in the same tradition was their special
call-to-lunch song.

Only little Eightah failed to come, for she
was stuck in a tree.

The whole family went to her rescue.

When Eightah was out of danger,

they sat silently where they were
and thought about the peaceful countryside.

"Stay up here for a minute," said Papa Minus.
"I have another surprise in the car."

And back he came with a bag.
"Here it is, the latest thing! A portable tree house!"

The family split into two groups.
Pulling from the left were Secondus, Harry,
Thirdly, Fifthmore, and Sevenor.

Pulling from the right were Firsterix, Sixus,
Fourthem, Eightah, and Mary.
Soon the house was finished.

When the house was full of little Minuses,
the branch supporting it began bending
toward the ground.

Now they were all in great danger.

"We had better build the house on the ground,"
said Harry. "I'm sorry about losing that view."
"Don't worry about the view," said Mary.
"I can solve that."

With the house ready once again,
they quickly ate the picnic meal.

Mary had brought her around-the-corner periscope.
This way they all could look at the beautiful view
just as if they were in the tree.

After such a busy day,
the Minuses got ready for bed.
Sweet dreams, Family Minus!

ABOUT THE AUTHOR/ILLUSTRATOR

Fernando Krahn, an accomplished picture-book artist and author, is also a successful cartoonist and filmmaker. His memorable characters are the result of a highly individualistic blend of fine draftsmanship, wit, and graphic charm. Born in Chile, Mr. Krahn and his family now live in Spain.